ALMOST ZERO

A **DYAMONDE DANIEL** Book

Also by Nikki Grimes

Jazmin's Notebook

Bronx Masquerade

The Road to Paris

Make Way for Dyamonde Daniel

Rich: A Dyamonde Daniel Book

ALMOST ZERO

A **DYAMONDE DANIEL** Book

Nikki Grimes

illustrated by
R. Gregory Christie

G. P. Putnam's Sons
An Imprint of Penguin Group (USA) Inc.

G. P. PUTNAM'S SONS
A division of Penguin Young Readers Group.
Published by The Penguin Group.
Penguin Group (USA) Inc., 375 Hudson Street, New York, NY 10014, U.S.A.
Penguin Group (Canada), 90 Eglinton Avenue East, Suite 700, Toronto, Ontario
M4P 2Y3, Canada (a division of Pearson Penguin Canada Inc.).
Penguin Books Ltd, 80 Strand, London WC2R 0RL, England.
Penguin Ireland, 25 St. Stephen's Green, Dublin 2, Ireland
(a division of Penguin Books Ltd.).
Penguin Group (Australia), 250 Camberwell Road, Camberwell, Victoria 3124,
Australia (a division of Pearson Australia Group Pty Ltd).
Penguin Books India Pvt Ltd, 11 Community Centre, Panchsheel Park,
New Delhi - 110 017, India.
Penguin Group (NZ), 67 Apollo Drive, Rosedale, North Shore 0632, New
Zealand (a division of Pearson New Zealand Ltd).
Penguin Books (South Africa) (Pty) Ltd, 24 Sturdee Avenue, Rosebank,
Johannesburg 2196, South Africa.
Penguin Books Ltd, Registered Offices: 80 Strand, London WC2R 0RL, England.

Library of Congress Cataloging-in-Publication Data
Grimes, Nikki. Almost zero : a Dyamonde Daniel book / Nikki Grimes ; illustrated
by R. Gregory Christie. p. cm. Summary: Dyamonde is angry at her mother for
not buying her the shoes she wants, but when she finds out that a classmate has
it a lot worse, she is determined to help. [1. Voluntarism—Fiction. 2. Conduct of
life—Fiction. 3. Schools—Fiction.] I. Christie, Gregory, 1971– ill. II. Title.
PZ7.G88429Al 2010 [Fic]—dc22 2010002282
ISBN 978-0-399-25177-1
1 3 5 7 9 10 8 6 4 2

For Barb Wallingford,
beloved mother of Adam, Brian, and Emily,
devoted teacher, and passionate lover of literature
—N.G.

For Ruth Edwards
—R.G.C.

Contents

Dyamonde is always on the
lookout for a friend in need!

The World of
Dyamonde Daniel

Dyamonde Daniel

This third-grader is smart enough
to know she should never tell her
mom what to do . . . but sometimes
she forgets. Fortunately, Dyamonde
can also use that big brain of hers
to come up with a plan when a
friend needs her help.

Free

He's Dyamonde's best friend, and even
though she doesn't always listen to his
advice, he always comes through for
her when she needs him.

Damaris

A great friend with a big heart, she's
also the best writer Dyamonde knows.
She adds poetic flair to any project, and
the two girls make a great team!

Isabel

She has a cool white streak in her hair that makes Dyamonde a little jealous. But when Isabel's family needs help, Dyamonde is determined to make sure they get it.

Tameeka

This stylish girl likes to show off her expensive clothes, and sometimes she's not very nice, but who knows—she might end up surprising Dyamonde.

Dyamonde's mom

She loves Dyamonde and works hard to give her everything she needs—but sometimes they don't agree on the difference between "want" and "need"!

1.
Sneaker Heaven

Dyamonde Daniel was not jealous of anyone. Except maybe Isabel, a girl in her class who was born with a streak of white in her hair that Dyamonde thought was too cool. Plus Isabel was cute, with dimples you could swim in, which didn't help matters.

Good thing I'm a better dresser,

1

Dyamonde sometimes thought to herself. Not that she'd ever say that out loud. Dyamonde thought being mean was the most uncool thing in the universe.

Monday morning, she and Isabel were standing in front of school talking when Tanya, Tylisha and Tameeka, the three T's, paraded past like models on a runway, showing off their new matching hoodies.

Oh, puleeze, thought Dyamonde.

Free snuck up behind the three T's, swishing his bony hips like he was a model too.

"Stop it, Free!" said Dyamonde,

trying not to laugh. Free straightened up just as Tameeka turned around. Isabel covered her laughter by bending down to retie her shoes, and Dyamonde lowered her smiling eyes.

"Cool sneaks!" said Dyamonde, noticing Tameeka's pink high-top sneakers.

"Thanks," said Tameeka.

"Those come in red?" asked Dyamonde. Red was her favorite color.

"Yeah," said Tameeka. "I saw some red ones at Sneaker Heaven."

Dyamonde's face fell. Sneaker

3

Heaven was expensive. She really liked those sneakers, though. Tameeka could tell.

"Why don't you tell your mom to buy you some?"

"Huh?"

"Tell her. That's what I do. If I need something, I tell my mom to get it."

"You're kidding, right?" said Dyamonde. Who ever heard of telling your mom what to do?

"No. I'm serious. I tell her *nice,* but, you know. She's my *mom,* and it's her *job* to get me whatever I need."

4

Well, thought Dyamonde, *I guess that's true.*

"You should try it," said Tameeka. "Just tell her you need some red high-tops. That's it."

Dyamonde nodded. Damaris and Free, who were standing nearby, traded looks.

"Don't do it, Dy," said Free. "If you do, your mom will pop you one. Guaranteed."

"He's right, Dy," Damaris chimed in.

"Oh, puleeze!" said Dyamonde. "Shows how much you know. She'd never do that. My mom doesn't

5

believe in coral . . . in corporate . . . my mom doesn't believe in hitting."

"Okay. But don't say I didn't warn you."

Dyamonde shrugged him off.

That evening, when her mom was in the living room reading the funnies, Dyamonde marched in and cleared her throat.

"Mom, I need some red high-top sneakers."

"Is that a question?" asked Mrs. Daniel.

"Not exactly," said Dyamonde. "I really need you to get me some red high-top sneakers."

"Dyamonde, the three pairs of sneakers you already have are just fine," said Mrs. Daniel.

This isn't working, thought Dyamonde. *I must not be doing it right.*

"No, they are not fine!" said Dyamonde, raising her voice. She crossed her arms and threw her shoulders back. "I need red ones, and you have to get them for me."

"Excuse me?"

"You're my mother, and mothers have to take care of their children, and you have to get them for me. It's your job!" Dyamonde was practically shouting.

Mrs. Daniel was silent for a moment.

"Is that so?" she said, in a quiet voice.

"Yes, that's so," said Dyamonde. Only now she wasn't so sure. Her mom's voice was scary-soft.

"I see," said Mrs. Daniel.

Dyamonde gulped.

"Well, let me give it some thought."

"Okay," squeaked Dyamonde.

Dyamonde stood in the middle of the living room floor, bouncing from one foot to the other. She didn't know what to do next.

"You can set the table for dinner," said her mom. "That is, if you don't *mind*."

Oh, boy, thought Dyamonde. *I hope I'm not in big trouble.*

For the rest of the evening, she watched her mom, waiting to see if she was going to announce some punishment. But nothing happened. Still, Dyamonde had a hard time falling asleep that night.

Tuesday morning, Dyamonde tiptoed around the house, careful not to disturb her mom. They ate breakfast together, like any other day. And like any other day, her mom smiled when Dyamonde said good-bye.

Free was on the stoop waiting for Dyamonde when she came out of the building.

"Well?" asked Free, getting right to the point. "Did you do it?"

"Uh-huh," said Dyamonde.

"And?"

"And what?"

"Did she pop you one?"

Dyamonde rolled her eyes. "I told you, my mom doesn't believe in that stuff."

"So, how'd it go?"

"Okay, I guess," said Dyamonde.

I think it did.

I hope it did.

All Dyamonde knew for sure was that she didn't want to talk about it.

"You choose what to read for your book report?" she asked Free.

"Huh? Oh, yeah! I found this great book on Jackie Robinson."

Baseball, thought Dyamonde. *It figures.*

Once Free started talking baseball, he forgot about everything else. That left Dyamonde alone with her thoughts, and that was just fine.

The rest of the school day was normal. And by the end of it, Dyamonde had stopped worrying about whether her mom was mad at her or not. But when she got home, she was in for a big surprise.

2. Robbed

"Mom!" screamed Dyamonde. "Somebody robbed our house!"

"Stop screaming, child," said Mrs. Daniel. "The whole building can hear you."

"But somebody robbed our house!" said Dyamonde.

"No," said Mrs. Daniel in a calm voice. "They didn't."

"But—"

"Is the television gone?" asked Mrs. Daniel. "Or the CD player?"

Dyamonde looked around the living room. The TV and CD player were there, exactly where they should be.

"If our house wasn't robbed, then how come all my clothes are missing?"

And they were. The hall closet where Dyamonde kept her clothes was bare. The hangers were naked as a newborn. The dresser drawers were empty, each hanging open like the tongue from a dog's

16

mouth. The only thing left in the closet was some underwear, a pair of neatly folded pajamas, and one pair of just-washed fuzzy bunny slippers. Those sat atop the dresser.

"What happened to all my clothes?" asked Dyamonde.

Her mom fell into her old recliner, exhausted. She slowly kicked off her shoes, one at a time. She removed her watch, carefully placed it on the end table beside her and made herself comfy before she finally spoke.

Dyamonde felt like shaking her.

"Nobody stole your clothes,

Dyamonde," said her mom. "I packed them up and took them away."

"Huh?" Dyamonde did not believe her ears.

"Last night, you told me it was my job, as your mother, to give you what you need. Remember?"

Dyamonde felt sick to her stomach. She didn't like where this was going.

"So, I thought about it. And you were right. It is my job to give you a roof over your head, a safe place to sleep, food to eat and clothes to wear."

Dyamonde nodded. So far, so good.

"But guess what, Dyamonde. Nowhere does it say I have to give you *more* than you need. So I've decided, from now on, I'll give you exactly what you need and nothing more."

Dyamonde's heart pounded against her chest.

"There are no clothes in my closet except pajamas. I can't go to school wearing pajamas."

"No, you can't," her mother agreed.

"Then what am I supposed to wear tomorrow?"

"The same clothes you wore today," said Mrs. Daniel. Then she picked up the television remote and switched on the news.

Dyamonde's feet were glued to the living room floor, and her mouth hung wide open.

"Better close your mouth, or you'll catch flies," said her mom.

Dyamonde balled her fists and made a choking sound. Then she ran to the bathroom, slammed the door as hard as she could and plopped down on the side of the bathtub.

"I hate you, I hate you, I hate you!" muttered Dyamonde. Then she went to the sink and turned the water on full blast to cover the sound of her crying.

3. Mean Mom
and the
Mustard Stain

Wednesday morning, Dyamonde stomped and banged doors as loudly as she could, hoping to make her mom as mad as she was. But it didn't work. Her mom pretended not to notice.

"Big deal," Dyamonde muttered to herself. "So what if I have to wear the same stupid clothes

I had on yesterday. I don't care." Dyamonde's lie sounded pretty weak, even to herself.

Dyamonde pulled on her red T-shirt, which had a quarter-size mustard stain on it from the bite of hot dog Free gave her at lunch the day before.

"Shoot!" said Dyamonde.

She went to the kitchen sink, squirted dishwashing liquid on a sponge and dabbed at the stain. That only made the spot bigger.

"Crumb!"

Now she was really mad, but there was nothing she could do

about it. She had to leave for school soon or she'd be late. She zipped on her blue jean skirt, pulled on her striped vest and hoped the spot didn't show too much. She pulled on her stinky socks, which slouched more than clean ones did, and Dyamonde hated that.

"Get a move on!" called her mom.

Dyamonde sucked her teeth and knelt to tie her white sneakers.

Her mom was at the door, holding it open.

"Have a good day," said Mrs. Daniel.

Dyamonde looked at her mom

like she was crazy, but she didn't say a word. She figured her mouth had gotten her in enough trouble already.

"What took you so long?" asked Free as soon as she hit the stoop. "I almost went to school by myself."

"Then why didn't you?" snapped Dyamonde.

"Hey!" said Free. "What's wrong with you?"

"Nothing," said Dyamonde. "I'm sorry."

Free scratched his head.

The two walked awhile in silence. Free studied Dyamonde when she wasn't looking.

"What happened to your shirt?" asked Free.

Dyamonde's hand flew to the spot, still wet, peeking out from behind the vest.

"It had a mustard stain. I tried to wash it, but . . ." Dyamonde's voice trailed off.

"So why didn't you just put on a different shirt?" asked Free.

"BECAUSE I DIDN'T, THAT'S WHY," yelled Dyamonde.

"Geez!" said Free, jumping back. "Alls I did was ask you a question!"

"I know," said Dyamonde, calmer. "I guess I don't feel like talking right now."

"Okay by me," said Free, throwing his hands up. "Later, then." Without saying another word, Free jogged ahead, leaving Dyamonde to herself.

Dyamonde growled, mad at herself for chasing her friend away, even madder at Tameeka for her stupid idea.

God, thought Dyamonde, *let Tameeka be sick today, just a little, just so she has to stay home. I don't think I could stand to see her right now.*

4. Almost Zero

Naturally, the first person Dyamonde saw when she arrived at school was Tameeka in her pink high-top sneakers.

"Hey, Dyamonde," she said. "You get your red high-tops yet?"

Dyamonde wished her eyes were balls of fire. That way, she could burn Tameeka to the ground.

31

"No, I didn't get my red high-tops," snapped Dyamonde.

She turned to walk away just as Tameeka said, "Hey, didn't you wear that same shirt yesterday?"

Dyamonde fumed. She wanted to say, "You know how many clothes I have in my closet now, thanks to you? Almost zero!" But instead, Dyamonde turned on her heel and walked away.

Dyamonde avoided Tameeka for the rest of the day.

At lunch, she found a table all to herself. Everything was fine until some boy goofing off behind her knocked her elbow as she was about to take a sip of her milk. She ended up with more than a mouthful. Half the container spilled down her front.

"Rats!" said Dyamonde. Now her T-shirt was stained *and* sticky. She mopped up the milk with her napkin, which didn't help much. Her eyes filled with water, but Dyamonde refused to cry.

"Sorry," said the boy. Dyamonde glared at him. "Sorry," he said a second time, carrying his tray to a table as far away from Dyamonde as possible.

It's only milk, Dyamonde told herself. *It'll dry soon.* And it did.

Luckily, nobody besides Tameeka seemed to notice that she was wearing yesterday's outfit. At least, nobody else mentioned it.

By the end of the day, Dyamonde relaxed.

Maybe this won't be so bad after all, she thought.

But who was she kidding? The last thing Dyamonde wanted was a repeat of this day.

Walking home alone that afternoon, Dyamonde put that big brain of hers to work to figure a way out of her problem. *There has to be a way to get my clothes back,* thought Dyamonde. By the time she reached her front door, she had a plan.

Dyamonde was careful to be quiet as a mouse that evening. She did all her homework without complaining even once. When she was finished, she cleared her books away without being told and set the table for dinner. She put extra ice in her mom's glass and poured Mrs. Daniel's favorite diet soda. For herself she poured milk, like she was supposed to, instead of whining about wanting soda too, which is what she usually did.

After dinner, she cleared the dishes and scrubbed them until they were squeaky clean.

When Mrs. Daniel went to the living room to watch TV, Dyamonde ran ahead, grabbed the remote control and put it in her mother's hand. The minute her mom seemed settled comfortably, Dyamonde cleared her throat.

"Mommy," said Dyamonde— she never called her mother "Mommy" unless she wanted something—"Mommy, I was wondering. Could I have my clothes back now, please?"

"I'm sorry, honey," said her mom, pressing the channel changer on the remote. "What did you say?"

Dyamonde took a deep breath and tried again, using a voice sweeter than corn bread.

"I was wondering if I could have my clothes back now," said Dyamonde.

"Oh!" said Mrs. Daniel. "But I thought you understood. You already have all the clothes you need."

Dyamonde's smile slid sideways, melting quicker than a snowflake.

"But the clothes I have are all *dirty*," said Dyamonde, beginning to whine.

"Well, then," said her mom, looking up from the television, "I guess you'd better wash them. But you should do it soon, because it's almost your bedtime."

Dyamonde ground her teeth and made a sound halfway between a growl and a scream.

Her mom turned back to the television, and Dyamonde stomped off to the bathroom.

"Don't pour too much detergent in the sink," warned her

mother. "I don't want bubbles all over my bathroom floor."

Dyamonde slammed the door, ripped off her clothes and filled the sink to the brim. She poured in half a cup of soap powder and stuffed her shirt, panties and socks into the water to soak.

While Dyamonde waited for the soap to do its job, she stomped into the living room, stark naked, and stood there in the middle of the floor, daring her mom to say something.

"Sit down," said Mrs. Daniel. "You're blocking my view."

"Uhhhhh!" *What's the use?* thought Dyamonde. She glared at her mother and marched right back into the bathroom.

Dyamonde scrubbed her clothes until she thought they must be clean. Then she rinsed them out and hung them on a dryer rack in the bathtub. If they were still damp in the morning, she could always go to the basement laundry and toss them in the dryer.

She found herself yawning, more tired than she'd felt in a long time. She padded to the closet, got her pajamas and slipped them on.

41

Her mom switched off the television and went to her bedroom.

"Good night, Dyamonde," she said. But Dyamonde didn't answer. She just pulled out the sofa bed and crawled under the covers.

5. Suddenly Small

In class on Thursday, Dyamonde slumped down in her seat, trying her best to be invisible. She sat up straight, though, when the principal ducked into the room and handed Mrs. Cordell a piece of paper.

The teacher's eyes raced across the note in her hand. When she

45

reached the bottom of the page, she gave a little gasp and shook her head from side to side.

What is it? Dyamonde wondered.

"Class," said Mrs. Cordell, looking up now. "Some of you may have noticed that Isabel isn't here today. Last night, there was a terrible fire in the apartment house where her family lives, and their apartment was destroyed. Everyone got out safely, thank God, but the family lost everything they owned. When Isabel comes back to school next week, I want you all to be especially kind to her. And if you see her wearing the

46

same clothes several days in a row, don't tease her or make a big deal out of it. Those are probably the only clothes she has." She looked straight at Tameeka when she said it.

Tameeka squirmed in her seat. "What?" said Tameeka. "I didn't do anything."

"I am asking you all to be thoughtful," added Mrs. Cordell, looking around at the entire class. "Just imagine how you'd feel if it were you."

The teacher's words gave Dyamonde a twinge. She suddenly felt very small inside, making such a fuss about her mother packing up all her clothes. At least they hadn't burned up in a fire. Plus, Dyamonde believed that, sooner or later, she'd get them back. But what about Isabel?

"Is there gonna be a clothes drive or something?" asked Dyamonde. She forgot to raise her hand first, but Mrs. Cordell didn't seem to mind this one time.

"What do you mean?" asked the teacher.

"Are we gonna collect money or clothes or something?" That was the first thing Dyamonde thought of because that's what they did at her church when something bad like this happened to someone they knew.

"Well, Dyamonde, the school can't do anything officially. There are lots of people in the world who need things, and if the school chose one family to help, it wouldn't be fair to all the others."

"Well, that's just silly," said Dyamonde without thinking. "Fair has got nothing to do with it."

"Excuse me?" The teacher's voice rose.

"Ooooooh!" said one kid. "You must be itchin' to get sent to the principal's office!"

Dyamonde ignored him. "I mean, if we know somebody who needs help, we should help them, right?"

"I don't disagree, Dyamonde, but fund-raisers and clothing drives for individuals are not school policy. Of course, you're always free to do something on your own, if you like."

What can I do? Dyamonde asked herself. *I don't have any money.* Then it hit her. *But I do have clothes! Somewhere. Mom did a good job of hiding them. I just hope they're somewhere close by.*

6.
Tales out of School

The minute her mother walked in the door that night, Dyamonde ran to her.

"Mom! I need to go through my clothes—not for me this time, though. A girl in my school got burned out of her apartment and she doesn't have anything left."

"Slow down, Dyamonde. Let me get in the door first."

"Sorry." Dyamonde hopped from one foot to the other, impatient for her mother to set down her purse, kick off her shoes and settle into the recliner.

"That's better," Mrs. Daniel said, sighing. "Now, what were you saying?"

Dyamonde told her all about the announcement her teacher made in class and all about the crazy school policy about taking up collections.

"Mrs. Cordell said I could do something myself, if I wanted to. And I want to give Isabel some of my clothes because she doesn't have any at all, and we're the same size. So can I have my clothes back, just for a little while? You can take them away again. I just want to pick out a few for Isabel," said Dyamonde.

Dyamonde waited for her mother to say something. Instead, her mom just smiled.

"Why are you smiling?"

Mrs. Daniel ignored the question. "Let's get dinner going, then I'll see if I can remember what I did with all your clothes."

Dyamonde knew her mother was kidding about remembering where the clothes were, because she gave Dyamonde a wink when she said it.

"Tell me about this girl," said Mrs. Daniel, over dinner.

Dyamonde shrugged. "She's a girl in my class I talk to sometimes. She's got this great white streak in her hair, and she's nice. I don't really know her as much as I know Free and Damaris, though."

"I see."

"You don't have to know somebody to help them. Right?"

Dyamonde's mother flashed that slow smile again, saying nothing.

After the dishes were washed and put away, Mrs. Daniel slipped out of the apartment. A few minutes later, the doorbell rang.

"Oh, puleeze!" said Dyamonde, rolling her eyes to the ceiling. "Mom forgot her keys. Again."

When Dyamonde opened the front door, she found her mother and their neighbor, Mrs. King, both juggling armloads of boxes.

"Say hello to Mrs. King," said Mrs. Daniel.

"Good evening, Mrs. King," said Dyamonde.

"Mrs. King was kind enough to store these boxes in her extra bedroom closet."

So that's where they were, thought Dyamonde.

"Well, come on! Give us a hand," said her mom.

Dyamonde was happy to grab one of the boxes.

Once all of the cartons were neatly stacked in front of

Dyamonde's closet, Mrs. King said good night and left.

"Whew!" said Mrs. Daniel. "Glad that's done. I'm off duty for the rest of the night, but you can go ahead and put away whatever clothes you've decided to keep for yourself."

Raising an eyebrow, Dyamonde turned to her mother. "But I thought—"

"You thought I'd take your things away again, after you set aside clothes for Isabel?"

Dyamonde nodded.

"No, honey. It's clear you've learned the lesson: Everything we have is a gift. I'm just pleased you've found it in your heart to share some of your gifts with others."

Dyamonde threw her arms around her mother's waist and squeezed tighter than she ever had before.

7.
Good-bye, Clothes

Dyamonde sorted her clothes quickly, saying good-bye to some of her favorite shirts and pants. She held up a red cardigan her mom had given her one Christmas. Dyamonde ran a hand over the soft sleeves and sighed.

I love this sweater, thought Dyamonde. *But it's not like I don't*

63

have plenty more. And if I love it, then Isabel will too.

Dyamonde folded the sweater and added it to the pile.

Hey, thought Dyamonde, *now Isabel will be as good a dresser as me!* Dyamonde wasn't sure how she felt about that. She liked looking special. What would it feel like to see Isabel in some of her favorite clothes? Dyamonde gave it some thought. *It'll be okay,* Dyamonde decided. *Nobody looks as good wearing my clothes as I do!*

Little by little, the stack of clothes for Isabel grew. Dyamonde folded them carefully, then pushed them into a brown paper shopping bag. She sighed, feeling pretty good about herself. But not for long.

What about Isabel's brothers and sisters? wondered Dyamonde. *And what about her mom and dad? They need clothes too, and I don't have anything to fit them.* Dyamonde had never met them, but Isabel talked about her family all the time.

Dyamonde went to the kitchen for a glass of water. She sat at the table for a minute, sipping her water and thinking. Then she jumped up, grabbed her loose-leaf

notebook, ripped out a page and
started writing.

Where to Find More Clothes:

<u>Men's Clothes</u>
• Free's dad
• Mrs. King's grown son (he's
away at college and won't miss
anything anyway)
• The building super

<u>Women's Clothes</u>
• Mom
• Mrs. Freeman
• Ms. Gracie Lee

<u>Boys' Clothes</u>
• Free
• His little brother, Booker

<u>Girls' Clothes</u>
• Me
• The Three T's?

Dyamonde looked at the list long enough to know that she needed a lot more people on it. The problem was most of the people she knew were at school, and the school would not sponsor a clothing drive.

But what if I collected clothes outside of the school building? wondered Dyamonde.

The way she figured, that would probably be okay. Now all she had to do was let everybody know.

Dyamonde ripped another page from her loose-leaf and got busy.

ISABEL MARTINEZ CLOTHING DRIVE

(This is NOT a school clothing drive, in case you were wondering.)

In case you haven't heard,
Isabel Martinez and her
family got burnt out of
their apartment. They lost
everything, and that includes
clothes.

You can help. Donate some
of your clothes so they'll
have something to wear.

Thank you.

Signed,
Dyamonde Daniel

Dyamonde's handwriting was not the best, so she wrote it out again, slowly this time.

"There," said Dyamonde when she was done. "Now all I need is a hundred more copies. Ugh!"

Dyamonde remembered seeing a copy machine at the library. Maybe she could—

"Dyamonde?" said Mrs. Daniel.

"Yeah? I mean, yes?"

"Finish putting those clothes away. It's getting late."

"Okay," said Dyamonde. "I'm almost done."

I'll try the library tomorrow,

thought Dyamonde. *I better ask Damaris to read my flyer first to make sure it's okay. After all, she did win a writing contest.*

"What's taking you so long?" asked Mrs. Daniel.

"Just have to put my shoes away," said Dyamonde.

Shoes! Isabel needs shoes! thought Dyamonde. *How could I forget?*

"Mom? Do we have another shopping bag?"

8. A Good Cause

Dyamonde slipped the flyer to Damaris under the table during lunch on Friday.

"Read it when you get a chance," whispered Dyamonde. "Let me know if I need to fix anything, 'cause I need to make lots of copies and I don't want all those copies to have mistakes in them."

Damaris peeked at the flyer, then put it away before anyone could see it.

"How are you making copies?"

"Library," said Dyamonde. "They've got a copy machine."

"Yeah, but they charge a lot."

Dyamonde shrugged. "It's not like I have a choice. I can't make all the copies by hand."

"Yeah, but how are you going to pay for them?"

"I'll use my allowance until it runs out."

"Oh. Yeah," said Damaris, looking away.

Dyamonde bit her lip. *Shoot!* she thought. *I forgot. Damaris doesn't get an allowance anymore. Her mom can't afford it.*

"Anyway," said Dyamonde, trying to change the subject, "it won't matter how many copies I make if the writing is all wrong. You're the only writing-contest winner I know, so you gotta help me."

"All right. Quit bugging!" said Damaris, but she was smiling when she said it. "I'll get it back to you later."

"Get what back?" asked Free, plopping his lunch tray down next to them.

"Wouldn't you like to know?" said Damaris. She winked at Dyamonde and they both laughed out loud, enjoying their secret for a little while longer.

"Here," said Damaris, handing Dyamonde a piece of paper that afternoon when school let out.

"Wow," whispered Dyamonde, reading the announcement for the clothing drive. After Damaris rewrote it, the announcement was practically poetry.

ISABEL MARTINEZ
CLOTHING DRIVE

Isabel is
a stranger,
a classmate,
a friend.
Her family needs the shirt
 off your back.
They lost theirs in a fire.
Do you have one to spare?
Do you even care?
Donate clothes outside of
 school.

77

If you can't find us,
  you're not really looking.
But we are.
We're looking to see
if your heart is small as a
  pea,
or big as the sky.

Dyamonde read the announcement again and smiled.

Now tell me that isn't great poetry, thought Dyamonde.

The girls raced to the public library to use the computer.

Once the announcement was typed up, they realized they could fit three on a page. That meant three times as many copies!

Dyamonde chose the lettering, something official-looking but bold. When she was done, she hit print and waited forever for the printer to spit it out. Then, copy in hand, she dug her $3.50 out of her pocket and went to the reference desk for change.

"We need change for this too, please," said Damaris, plunking a five-dollar bill on the counter. Dyamonde's jaw dropped. Damaris never had that much money.

"That's what's left over from my poetry-contest prize," explained

Damaris. "I gave most of it to my mom, but she made me keep ten dollars for myself. This is what's left."

"But don't you want to use it for something fun?" asked Dyamonde.

Damaris shrugged. "You can't buy much with five dollars these days," she said. "Besides, this is for a good cause."

Dyamonde smiled and gave her friend's shoulder a squeeze. After that, she was all business.

"Okay. We've got $8.50. Each copy costs 15 cents. That means we have enough for"—Dyamonde did the math in her head—"56 copies."

"Times three," said Damaris. "Remember, there are three announcements per page."

"Right! So that makes it 168 copies. Whew! We better get started."

Dyamonde placed the page on the copier glass and started feeding in the coins, one quarter at a time. The machine was old and cranky. It whined and clunked with every copy it spit out. The whole process took forever. Before long, there was a line of people behind

Dyamonde and Damaris, waiting their turn to use the copier.

When the reference librarian saw the long line, she walked up to Dyamonde.

"Let me help you," she said once Dyamonde told her how many copies she needed. "Give me the original page and what-ever change you have left."

Dyamonde handed over both.

"Wait there," the librarian told her, pointing to a table with chairs. Dyamonde nodded, stepping away from the copier so that the next person could use it. Meanwhile,

the librarian disappeared behind a door marked Staff Only.

Dyamonde and Damaris sat at the table whispering, wondering how long they'd have to wait. A few minutes later, the librarian returned holding a big stack of fliers. One look told Dyamonde there were way more than the 56 copies they had enough money to pay for.

The librarian laid the still-warm stack of copies on the table and leaned down to whisper in Dyamonde's ear.

"I threw in a few extra copies," she said. "It was for a good cause."

Dyamonde's eyes grew wide. She looked from the librarian to Damaris and back to the librarian. Dyamonde hardly knew what to say.

"Thank you," said Damaris for them both.

"Yes!" said Dyamonde, finding her voice again. "Thank you!"

"Now," said the librarian, "do you need some help cutting these?"

Dyamonde and Damaris both nodded. The librarian smiled, laid three pairs of scissors on the table, and pulled up a chair to join the girls.

That evening, Dyamonde called Free and told him all about her plans for a clothing drive, and about the flyer, and about how Damaris helped her with it. Free listened carefully, and when Dyamonde was done talking, Free said exactly the right thing.

"So when do I get my stack of flyers to hand out?"

9.
Spreading
the Word

Dyamonde wasted no time. She passed out flyers all weekend, sliding one underneath the front door of every apartment in her building. Free did the same in his building, and Damaris even handed out a few at the shelter where she lived. The way she figured, if she had five dollars stashed away, maybe somebody else had a dollar or two they'd like to give to help somebody else in need.

"If you never ask, you never know," said Damaris. "At least, that's what my mom is always saying."

On Monday, the three friends stood outside of the school and handed out flyers to students on their way to class. The three T's took flyers, curious to see what was going on. They stood a few feet away, reading, then Dyamonde watched as Tylisha threw hers on the ground. Her friends Tanya and Tameeka did the same.

"Hey!" snapped Dyamonde. "We worked hard on those. If you don't want yours, then give them back!"

Tameeka, looking a little embarrassed, bent down to pick them up. She walked over to Dyamonde and held the flyers out to her.

"Sorry," Tameeka whispered.

Dyamonde snatched the papers from her, keeping her thoughts to herself.

Shouldn't have wasted our flyers on the three T's in the first place, thought Dyamonde. *It's not like those fashion plates were about to give up any of their precious clothes.*

"Hurry up, Tameeka," called Tylisha. "We don't want to be late to class."

"Oh, puleeze!" said Dyamonde. The three T's were late all the time. *Forget them,* thought Dyamonde.

Dyamonde handed out flyers to the next batch of kids passing by.

"Can they use some scarves?" asked one girl. "I've got a bunch of them."

"They need some turtlenecks?" asked another girl.

"Who is Isabel?" asked a boy.

Before Dyamonde could answer, another boy tossed his copy

of the flyer in the air. "I ain't giving nobody the shirt off my back!"

"Nobody wants your ugly old shirt!" Free shot back.

Dyamonde just shook her head. She answered everyone's questions as best as she could and kept on handing flyers out until the first bell rang. Then she and her friends stuffed the remaining flyers in their backpacks and raced to class.

10. Pulling Together

That evening, a few of Dyamonde's neighbors stopped by with the first clothing donations. Dyamonde was so excited, she could burst. She called Free to tell him, but he had news of his own.

"Bet you could use a few men's shirts and shoes. How about

clothes for little kids? Yup! I got those too," said Free.

"It's working!" said Dyamonde. "My neighbors started bringing stuff too! Now if only the kids in school pitch in, we'll have plenty."

"Of course they will," said Free. "You just watch."

When Dyamonde left for school the following morning, Free was on the stoop waiting, like always. They started walking toward school, going slow so they'd have time to talk.

"So what are you gonna do with the clothes once you get them?"

Dyamonde looked at Free as if he'd sprouted two heads. "What do you think I'm going to do? Give them to Isabel's family, of course."

"I know *that*," snapped Free. "I mean, what are you going to put them in? I don't see you holding any bags."

"Oh," said Dyamonde. She'd forgotten about that. "Let me think."

Bags wouldn't hold enough. Boxes would be better, but how was she going to lug a bunch of heavy boxes all the way home from school?

"Got it!" said Dyamonde. "Wait for me."

Before Free could say anything, Dyamonde sprinted back to her building and ran inside. A few minutes later, she reappeared, pulling her mother's shopping cart behind her.

"Good idea!" said Free, waiting exactly where Dyamonde had left him. Free shrugged off his backpack and grabbed the cart from Dyamonde.

"What are you doing?" asked Dyamonde.

Free plunked his backpack into the cart.

"No sense in wasting this thing," he said. "I might as well give my back a rest."

Dyamonde smiled, shrugged off her own backpack and tossed it on top of Free's.

"You're right," said Dyamonde. "This is a good idea."

Free grunted, pulling the cart that was suddenly a whole lot heavier.

"Oh, quit groaning," said Dyamonde. "It's not that heavy."

Dyamonde felt silly dragging the shopping cart around, but she couldn't just leave it outside because someone might steal it. Lucky for her, Mr. Samson, the janitor, offered to lock it up in his closet until the end of the day.

Dyamonde, Damaris and Free took their places in front of the school after the last bell. They handed out flyers like they'd been doing for days, but this time Dyamonde stood next to the shopping cart, which had a sign on it reading "Clothing for Isabel."

Dyamonde was so busy handing out flyers, she didn't notice the first person drop something into the cart. It was a red vest—her favorite color! Dyamonde was almost tempted to grab it for herself, but she didn't. The vest was quickly followed by an assortment of T-shirts, jeans, pajamas—*Why didn't I think of pajamas?* Dyamonde wondered.

"Psst!" said Damaris. "Look who's coming!"

Dyamonde raised her eyes just in time to see her teacher approaching.

"Good afternoon, Dyamonde," said Mrs. Cordell.

Dyamonde froze. Was she in trouble? Was Mrs. Cordell going to take her to the principal's office for breaking school policy? Dyamonde felt herself starting to sweat.

"You know," said Mrs. Cordell, "it's a little too hot today for a jacket. Don't you think?"

Dyamonde's jaw dropped when the teacher slipped off her pretty blue jacket, folded it neatly and placed it in the shopping cart.

"That's better," said Mrs. Cordell.

"Thank you!" said Dyamonde, finding her voice.

"See you tomorrow," said Mrs. Cordell, walking away.

"Whew!" said Dyamonde,

breathing again. "That was scary."

The three T's hurried past without so much as glancing at the cart. When they reached the street corner, though, Tameeka turned around for a minute. She seemed to be staring at the cart, but Dyamonde couldn't figure out why.

Whatever, thought Dyamonde.

"I think that's it for today," said Free.

"Okay," said Dyamonde. "Let's get this stuff home."

11.
Brown Bag
Surprise

Dyamonde was amazed at how her idea had caught on. People from the neighborhood pitched in, offering stuff Dyamonde hadn't even asked for: dishes, pots and pans, towels—all sorts of things. She'd had to make a special trip to the supermarket just to get enough boxes to hold it all.

The stacks of boxes with all the collected clothing, school supplies and household goods were piling up in Dyamonde's living room. But her mother didn't even complain about the mess. In fact, each evening after she got home from work, she helped Dyamonde sort the donations.

Dyamonde couldn't wait to turn it all over to Isabel and her family. *One thing they'll know for sure,* thought Dyamonde. *They'll know people care.*

Damaris was right. She said there was love in those boxes. And there was.

Dyamonde pulled the shopping cart to school one last time. She was still hoping for a few pairs of shoes, and she told Free and Damaris to spread the word.

They set up the cart outside of school, as they had every day, and waited as students and teachers piled out. Most people who were interested had already given their donations. But one teacher dropped off some leather loafers that should fit Isabel's father, and a boy threw in some sneakers.

Dyamonde bent down to re-move the "Clothing for Isabel" sign from the cart, ready to call it a day.

"Am I too late?" asked a famil-iar voice. Dyamonde stood up to find Tameeka.

"Too late for what?" asked Dyamonde.

"The clothing drive."

"No," said Dyamonde, won-dering what Tameeka was up to. "We're still here, aren't we?"

"Good," said Tameeka. "Then here." She handed Dyamonde a brown paper sack and took off down the street before Dyamonde could say anything.

"What's that?" asked Free, pointing to the paper bag.

"Beats me," said Dyamonde. "Probably some old junk Tameeka doesn't need anymore."

Dyamonde placed the sack into the cart without bothering to look inside. Later, when she got home and had unloaded the cart, she sat on the sofa, opened the paper bag and reached inside. She pulled out a pair of nearly new pink high-top sneakers.

"I don't believe it," said Dyamonde.

She stared at the sneakers, shaking her head, thinking back to the day she first saw them on Tameeka's feet, how badly she'd wanted a pair, how much trouble she'd gotten herself into trying to force her mom to buy her a pair (in red, of course!). It seemed so silly now. She didn't really need those sneakers, and neither did Tameeka. But Isabel did, and now she'd have them.

Dyamonde fell against the sofa

cushions, sighing. She didn't need to switch on the television, or lose herself in a book, or even call anyone. She just closed her eyes and let the warm feeling inside wrap its arms around her.

Dyamonde had heard that it was better to give than to receive. She'd never believed it, though. Until now.

Born and raised in New York City, **Nikki Grimes** began composing verse at the age of six and has been writing ever since. She is the critically acclaimed author of numerous award-winning books for children and young adults, including Coretta Scott King Award winner *Bronx Masquerade*, Coretta Scott King Honor winner *The Road to Paris* and *New York Times* bestseller *Barack Obama: Son of Promise, Child of Hope* (illustrated by Bryan Collier). In addition to a Coretta Scott King Award and four Coretta Scott King Honors, her work has received accolades such as the NCTE Award for Excellence in Poetry for Children, *Booklist* Editors' Choice, ALA Notable, Bank Street College Book of the Year, *Horn Book* Fanfare, *American Bookseller* Pick of the List, Notable Social Studies Trade Book, NAACP Image Award Finalist, and the Golden Dolphin Award, an award given by the Southern California Children's Booksellers Association in recognition of an author's body of work. She lives in Corona, California.

Visit her at www.nikkigrimes.com.